Goldilocks and the Three Bears

Stories adapted by Shirley Jackson
Illustrated by Jeannette Slater
Series designed by Jeannette Slater

Published in Great Britain by Egmont World Limited,
Deanway Technology Centre, Wilmslow Road,
Handforth, Cheshire SK9 3FB
Printed in Germany
ISBN 0 7498 4362 4

chair
bear
porridge

Goldilocks
bed

Once upon a time,
the three bears went
out.

Goldilocks came.

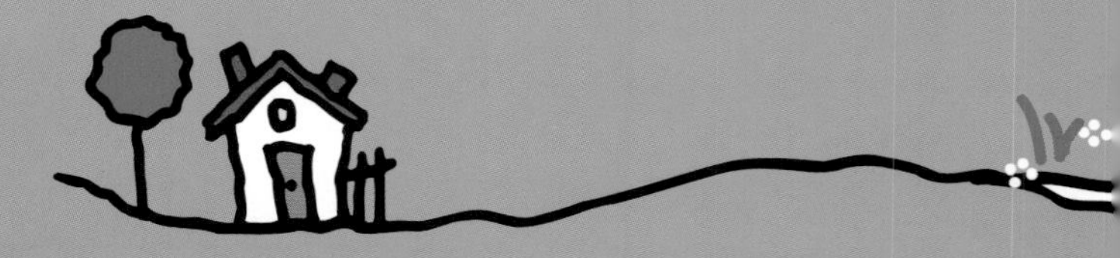

new words **bears out**

Goldilocks saw some porridge.

"This porridge is too hot," said Goldilocks.

"This porridge is too cold," said Goldilocks.

new words **saw** **This** **too** **hot** **cold**

"This porridge is just right," said Goldilocks.

Goldilocks saw three chairs.

new words **just right chairs**

“This chair is too high,” said Goldilocks.

“This chair is too low,” said Goldilocks.

new words **high** **low**

“This chair is just right,” said Goldilocks.

Goldilocks saw three beds.

new word **beds**

“This bed is too hard,” said Goldilocks.

“This bed is too soft,” said Goldilocks.

new words **hard** **soft**

"This bed is just right,"
said Goldilocks.

The bears came home.

no new words

“Who has been eating my porridge?” said Daddy Bear.

“Who has been eating my porridge?” said Mummy Bear.

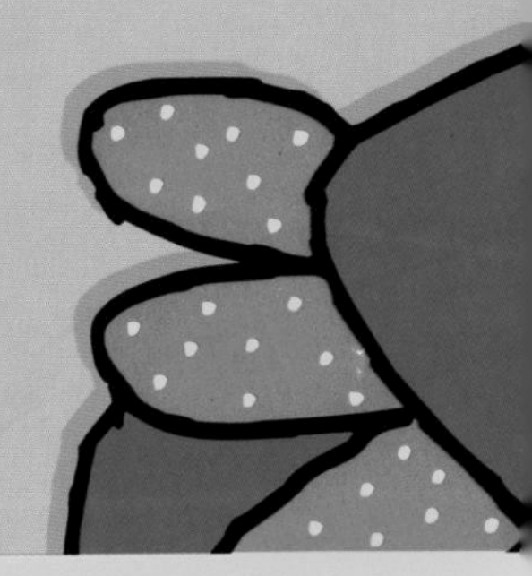

new words **has been eating Daddy Mummy**

"Look at **my** porridge!"
said Baby Bear.

new words **Look at Baby**

"Who has been sitting in my chair?" said Daddy Bear.

"Who has been sitting in my chair?" said Mummy Bear.

"Look at **my** chair," said Baby Bear.

new word **sitting**

"Who has been
sleeping in my bed?"
said Daddy Bear.

"Who has been
sleeping in my bed?"
said Mummy Bear.

"Look at **my** bed!" said
Baby Bear.

new word **sleeping**

Goldilocks looked at
the three bears.

new word **looked**

Goldilocks jumped out of bed and ran away.